This vacation Bible school inspired the Bible Buddy named Mack. Mack is a rhinoceros. In God's creation, rhinos are nearing extinction through no fault of their own, which is unfair. Mack reminds kids that, even when life is unfair,

God is good!

Best of Buddies
That's Not Fair! Doesn't God Care?
Written by **JEFF WHITE**   *Illustrated by* **JULIE MELLAN**

Group | **lifetree**™

MyLifetree.com
Loveland, CO

Copyright © 2019 Group Publishing, Inc./0000 0001 0362 4853
Lifetree™ is an imprint of Group Publishing, Inc. Visit our website: **group.com**

Author: Jeff White
Illustrator: Julie Mellan
Chief Creative Officer: Joani Schultz
Senior Editor: Candace McMahan
Designer: RoseAnne Sather
Assistant Editor: Cherie Shifflett

Scripture quotations are taken from the Holy Bible, New Living Translation, copyright © 1996, 2004, 2015 by Tyndale House Foundation. Used by permission of Tyndale House Publishers, Inc., Carol Stream, Illinois 60188. All rights reserved.

Library of Congress Cataloging-in-Publication Data
Names: White, Jeff, 1968- author. | Mellan, Julie, illustrator.
Title: That's not fair! Doesn't God care? / written by Jeff White ;
   illustrated by Julie Mellan.
Description: Loveland, CO : Group Publishing, Inc., [2019] | Series: Best of
   buddies.

Identifiers: LCCN 2018041799 (print) | LCCN 2018048394 (ebook) | ISBN
   9781470757205 (ePub) | ISBN 9781470757250 (first American hardcover)
Classification: LCC PZ7.1.W443 (ebook) | LCC PZ7.1.W443 Th 2019 (print) | DDC
   [E]--dc23
LC record available at https://lccn.loc.gov/2018041799

978-1-4707-5725-0 (hardcover)
978-1-4707-5720-5 (ePub)

Printed in China.
001 China 1218

10 9 8 7 6 5 4 3 2 1   28 27 26 25 24 23 22 21 20 19

Mack was nibbling some grass
when a bird caught his eye.
He watched it dance in the breeze,
nearly high enough to kiss the sun.
"Why didn't God give me…what do they call
those things?" Mack muttered. "Wings."
The rhino scowled.
"That's not fair!"

Mack was feeling sorry for himself.
Then he started to feel lonely, too.
He watched the elephants huddle together.
They flapped their ears and swooshed their tails
as if they didn't have a care in the world.
"Why didn't God make me part of a…
a—what's the word?"
Mack murmured. "A herd."
The rhino sniffed.
"That's not fair!"

Mack stomped away. He stopped
when he saw a lion asleep on a mound.
He stared at the lion's fluffy fur.
"Why didn't God cover me with…
um—what does he wear?" Mack mumbled. "Hair."

The rhino snarled.
"That's not fair!"

Mack needed to cool down. He took a sip from the pond
and saw two fish below. They blew bubbles and wiggled
their fins in the crystal-clear water.
"Why couldn't God give me those…those—
what are those things on their skins?" Mack mused. "Fins."
The rhino snorted.
"That's not fair!"

Mack wanted to get away. So he started to run as fast as he could.
But all of a sudden he was being passed by a gazelle.
"What now? Why didn't God give me that kind of...
of—what do I need?" Mack moaned. "Speed."
The rhino snapped.
"That's not fair!"

"Everybody else has something I don't.
Everyone else can do something I can't.
**It's just not fair!
Doesn't God care?"**

Mack lost his temper. What a grump!
He charged at the nearest tree and
whacked it as hard as he could. THUMP!
The trunk shook, and the branches rattled.

Then Mack heard a tiny noise. "Pip!"
He looked down and saw a bush baby.
He had knocked her out of the tree.
"I'm sorry!" Mack said. "Are you okay?"

Bush Baby stared
up into Mack's huge face.
"Oh!" she gulped. "Someone as big as you
must be awfully hungry. If you don't mind,
may I say a prayer before you eat me?"

"Eat you?!" said Mack. "Eeeeww!
That's disgusting. I only eat grass."

"Wow!" Bush Baby said. "You've got
food everywhere you go! That must be so nice.
I only eat bugs—the creepy-crawly kind with
the wiggly legs. They're hard to find
and even harder to catch."

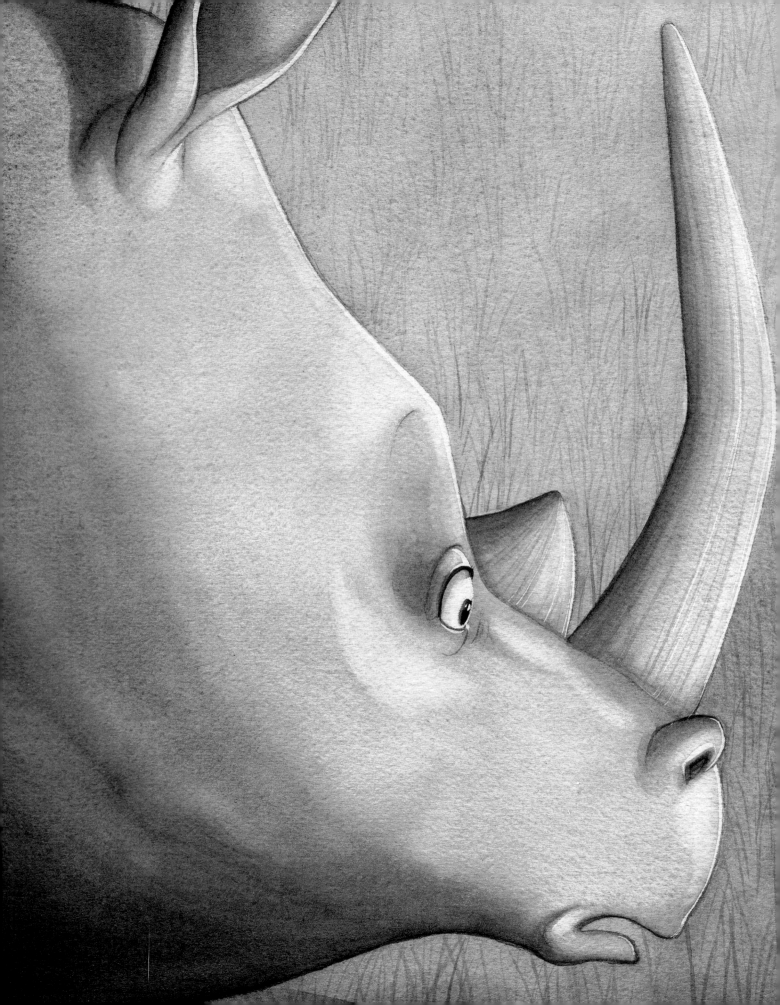

"And when I'm not busy looking for food," Bush Baby said, "I have to watch out so I don't *become* food! Hawks, crocs, cats, jackals, and hyenas would all love to have me for breakfast."

Then Bush Baby pointed her tiny finger at Mack. "Life can be hard for me. **But God has been so good to you!**"

"God's been good to *me*?
God made everyone else with something special—
fun stuff like feathers, fur, fins, and families.
All God made me is…um—what's it called?"
Mack moaned. "Bald."

Bush Baby grinned.
"Let me show you a thing or two about **just how good God can be.**"

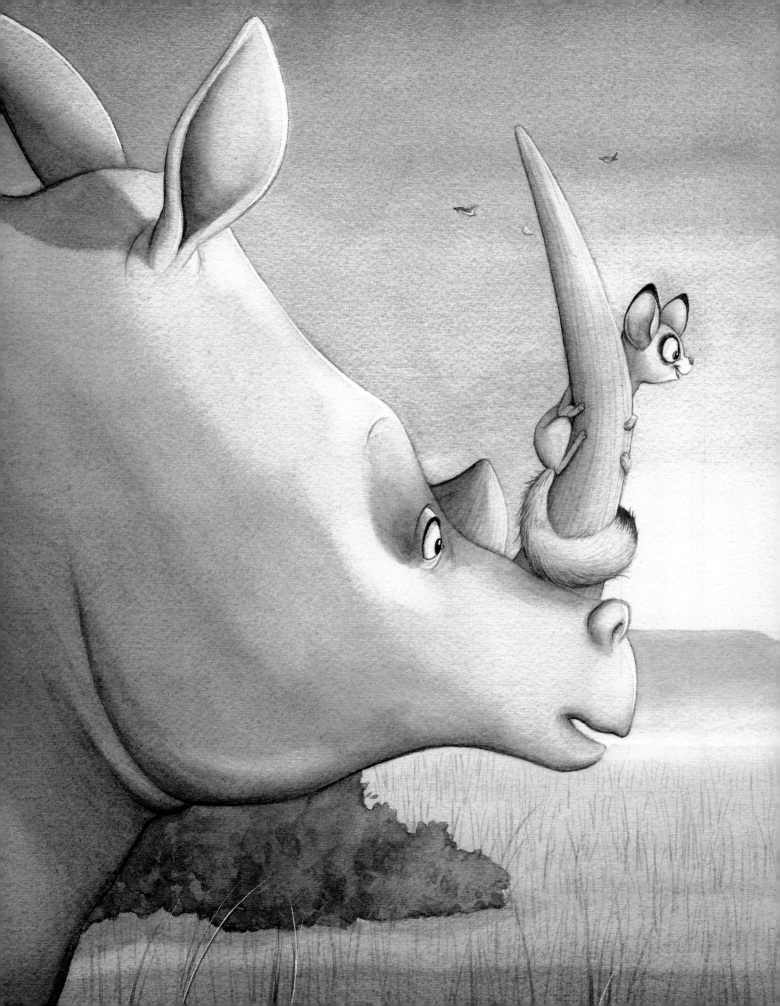

Bush Baby scanned the sky.
"God gave birds wings so
they can stay safe up in the air.
They thank God with their songs."

Bush Baby eyed the elephants.
"Those guys may be big, but they're safer
when they're together. They thank God
by being loyal to each other."

Bush Baby looked at the lion.
"God gave the lion a big, bushy mane
to keep his body strong. He thanks God
by protecting his family."

Bush Baby gazed at the gazelle.
"God blessed gazelles with speed so
they can leave their predators behind.
They honor God with their grace."

"And *you*! God made you big and strong and tough. He gave you all the food you could ever want. And God made you my new buddy," said Bush Baby.

Then she gave Mack the **biggest hug** her fluffy little body could give.

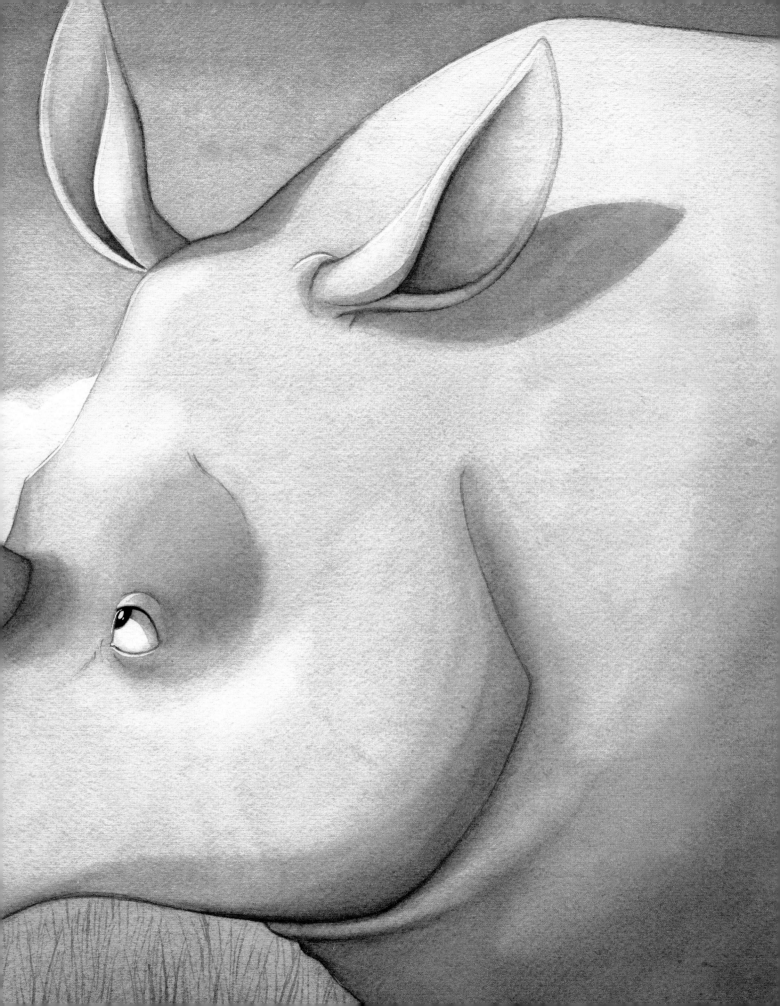

Mack smiled. "You're right.
Life's not always fair. But God always cares.
And he's made you my friend for...
um—what's the phrase?"
Mack said. **"All of my days."**

"The Lord is good, a strong refuge when trouble comes. He is close to those who trust in him."

(Nahum 1:7)

46726067R00021

FOR MORE INFORMATION AND GAMES

www.FeelingsAndDealings.com
https://twitter.com/FeelingDealing

www.GameOnFamily.com
https://twitter.com/GameOnFamilyCom

A NOTE FROM THE AUTHORS/PUBLISHER

Hi! Many thanks to you for supporting this book. I own the independent publishing house and small business that produced this book that I wrote with my husband Bryan. For small businesses, it's always exciting to see new orders come through. I celebrate each one and want to express my deep appreciation for trusting Game On Family with your purchase.

If you would, please consider leaving a review on Amazon. Reviews have an enormous impact on the discoverability, search ranking, and customer trust of products.

Enjoy your new book and please check out our companion "Feelings and Dealings: Color My Emotions" coloring book for ages 3-8 years and award-winning "Feelings and Dealings: An Emotions and Empathy Card Game" on Amazon!

With Gratitude,

Camille at Game On Family

FEELINGS AND DEALINGS GUIDE

feelings and dealings

F

FEEL

Allow and accept the child's feelings. This is not the time to "fix" the problem as emotions are neither right nor wrong. Ask the child to join you in taking slow, deep breaths. Repeat the word calm during exhales to re-center.

E

EDUCATE

What do you see, feel, and hear? Gather information by noting facial expressions, body language, and tone of voice. Ask questions to find out what s/he is experiencing and feeling. What impact is that experience having on him/her?

E

EMPATHIZE

Find out more. Use exploratory phrases such as, "I imagine that could make you feel...," or "I suppose that situation could make you think." Use exploratory words like could, possibly, maybe.

L

LISTEN

Teach the child to listen not only to words but also to the tone of voice by pointing out how they sound. By effectively monitoring and communicating, you'll improve your communication and collaboration.

I

INSPECT

Identify and challenge the thoughts behind the emotions. Inspect behavior in response to the event that triggered the feelings. Did s/he overreact? Is s/he blaming others for his/her emotions?

N

NARRATE

If the child can write, ask them to journal about their feelings to discharge them. They can narrate their story or write a letter. For young kids, ask them to color their feelings. They'll often feel better after visually expressing the emotion.

G

GAUGE

As the child improves at identifying emotions, begin gauging the size of the emotion. Ask him/her if the feeling is mild or extreme. Understanding the intensity or size of emotions aids in regulating them and knowing when they should seek help.

S

SELF-REGULATE

Support your child's self-regulatory skills by talking about and sticking to the daily schedule. Stay calm and firm when your child spirals emotionally. Teach and talk about feelings. Seek help if needed.

FeelingsAndDealings.com

We all have emotions,
None of them are bad.
Parents, kids, teachers, humans
Can feel sad one minute, then GLAD!

The next time you have strong feelings,
It can help a lot
To take 5 deep breaths and count to 10
Until the feeling of calm is caught!

Feelings come and go,
Like clouds moving across the skies.
You can tell a lot by looking at
People's faces, bodies, and eyes!

feelings and dealings

Z

is for ZIPPY

Zoe feels zippy,
Her smile and arms are wide.
She's so excited, screaming, "Yay!"
On the roller coaster ride.

Y

is for YUCKY

Yariv feels yucky
Disgusted with his tongue out.
But when eating at the table,
It's never polite to pout!

X

is for XOXO

Xavier feels XOXO,
He smiles as he cuddles his cat.
He loves to spend time with his family,
His cat loves the attention and a pat.

is for WORRIED

Will feels worried,
His best friend Sparky is his pet.
He bites his fingernails nervously
While Sparky sees the vet.

V

is for VULNERABLE

Veronica feels vulnerable
With a broken ankle, she can't do much.
Her body hunches in when she sees stairs,
And someone else must be her crutch.

U
is for UNCOMFORTABLE

Ursula feels uncomfortable,
She's afraid and doesn't want a shot!
Eyebrows raised and mouth stretched,
But she knows it will help a lot.

T

is for THANKFUL

Tim is thankful,
He got a present from a friend.
He smiles, and his heart feels warm,
He hopes this is a trend!

S

is for SAD

Sandy feels sad,
Her mouth curls down in a frown.
Her eyes droop and tear as she sees
Her ice cream flipped upside-down.

R
is for RELAXED

Rowan feels relaxed,
He smiles gently and reclines.
His body's loose. It's summertime,
It feels good when the sun shines!

Q

is for QUIET

Quincy is quiet,
Shhh. Don't make a sound!
A library is not a place,
For noisy kids to be found.

is for PROUD

Paul is proud,
He holds his chin up high.
He baked these muffins by himself -
Mmmmm, I'd like to try!

is for OVERWHELMED

Olivia feels overwhelmed,
Her hands upon her face show distress.
All this homework is due tomorrow,
Oh my, what a mess!

N

is for NERVOUS

Nelly is nervous,
A tense look upon her face.
She worries that making a mistake
Would be a big disgrace.

M

is for MAD

Mark is mad!
He grits his teeth and knits his brow,
Fighting with his sister,
He wants that controller NOW!

L

is for LONELY

Larry feels lonely,
Shoulders slumped and looking sad.
He eats his lunch all alone,
A friend would make him glad.

 is for KIND

Kira is kind,
Helping an old man at the store.
She feels so good and smiles,
It doesn't feel like a chore.

J is for JOYFUL

Jones feels joyful,
He grins widely with his bike.
We all feel happy when we exercise,
And spend time with people we like!

I is for IMPATIENT

Isaac feels impatient,
He makes a pouty-face.
Instead of waiting in this line,
He'd pick any other place!

is for HOPEFUL

Harriet feels hopeful,
Her friend happily waters a seed.
She clasps her hands and wishes,
For a flower, not a weed!

G

is for GUILTY

Greg feels guilty,
See his blushing face!
He hangs his head and looks down,
'Cause he broke his grandma's vase.

F

is for FRUSTRATED

Franchesca feels frustrated,
She lost a game to Phil.
She slaps her forehead and bites her lip,
But play again, she will!

E

is for EMBARRASSED

Evan feels embarrassed,
His red cheeks burn as he falls down.
When other kids laugh and tease him,
He feels shy and shows a frown.

D

is for DISTRACTED

Daisy is distracted
Staring intently at her phone.
She doesn't see Ruffles licking her plate,
Instead of chewing on his bone!

is for CONFUSED

Chloe feels confused
In a sandbox trying to play.
Her palms are up and eyebrows raised
Puzzled that Billy looks like Ray!

B

is for BORED

Britney feels bored,
Eyes half-closed and hand on chin.
It's dull to sell lemonade
When no one's buying in.

A

is for ASHAMED

Adam feels ashamed,
Looking down and away from dad.
He's sorry for what he did;
His actions were hurtful and bad.

Pay attention to your body,
How it moves when you feel.
Do you clench your hands in fists
Or stand up tall and squeal?

Let's name our emotions,
Through the alphabet.
We'll see kids dealing with feelings,
With family, friends, and pets!

Have you ever noticed
How someone shows a feeling
In their eyes, face, or body?
It can be quite revealing!

Have you ever seen
How raised brows or an open mouth look?
When we're in situations
We can read expressions like a book!

The A B C 's

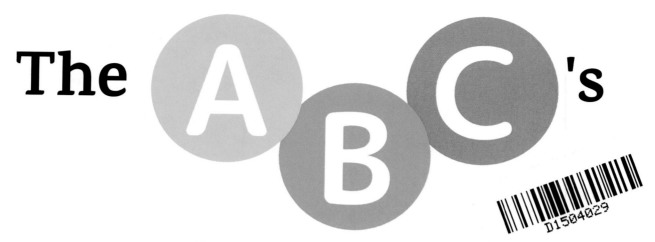

of Emotions

Camille Childs and Bryan Jones

Ofunlo Inc. dba Game On Family

To Jules and Rowan, our expressive kids. May you grow to be emotionally fluent, empathic, and compassionate adults. Special thanks to our moms: Camilla Childs for your moral support and Jane Bryan-Jones for your therapeutic and editorial expertise.

Paperback ISBN-13: 978-0-578-51482-6
eBook ISBN-13: 978-1-7331868-0-3
Library of Congress Control Number: 2019907425